William Baron

The Dutch Way of Toleration

Most Proper for Our English Dissenters

William Baron

The Dutch Way of Toleration
Most Proper for Our English Dissenters

ISBN/EAN: 9783337309152

Printed in Europe, USA, Canada, Australia, Japan

Cover: Foto ©Andreas Hilbeck / pixelio.de

More available books at **www.hansebooks.com**

T.HE

DUTCH *Way of* Toleration,

Moſt proper for our

ENGLISH DISSENTERS.

Written at the Requeſt of a Friend.

O ! Imitatores ſervum pecus.
Quo teneam vultus mutantem Protea Nodo?
Hor.

As free, and not uſing your Liberty for a Cloak of Malici-
ciouſneſs, &c. St. Pet: Ep. I. Ch. 2. V. 16.

𝕿𝖍𝖊 𝖘𝖊𝖈𝖔𝖓𝖉 𝕰𝖉𝖎𝖙𝖎𝖔𝖓.

LONDON,
Printed in the Year, 1699.

SECOND EDITION.

THe following Prospect of the Dutch Toleration, was taken upon the Spot more than Thirty Years since, where the Party had the Advantage of a full and frequent View, residing there a considerable time with one of Publick Character ; and tho' never before drawn upon Paper, much less expos'd to the Sight and Censure of the World, 'till the other day, yet is the representation no ways defective, for that ever since his Return, he hath had too much occasion to reflect upon the Impressions there fix'd, by comparing them with the many Mistakes, Impertinencies, and Abuses of their sordid Imitators here.

Two Things, more especially, have been both his Wonder and Indignation ; First, That having so good, so exact an Original of our own, we should affect so much to Copy after others : And then, Secondly, what they affect to Copy, are only the Weakest and Worst wrought Parts ; which, taken from the Symmetry of the rest, carry much of Deformity with them; having neither Art nor Order to set them off ; yet these, forsooth, must be daub'd upon our foremention'd Original, with design doubtless to expose, and utterly deface it in the End. A strange Infatuation this, that Men must be humour'd with a Religion, made up of such Uncouth, Dissonant Proportions, as Horace would allow of neither in Painting, nor Poetry; without a Spectatum Admissi, &c. although it ought to excite a quite contrary Passion in every good Christian.

And in regard hereunto, that our English World might understand what Mischiefs have already, and must farther accrew from such Patching, Daubing Designs, this little Piece stole abroad last Spring, amongst that numerous Spawn the Teeming Press casts forth; yet so, as neither Friend nor Foe, (but the Party who engag'd him) knew at first from what hand it came, the Designer having a just Suspicion, that as the Sincerity of his Plain-dealing Conversation had been more uneasie than he could first imagine, in this Time-serving Age, so those Prejudices might be still continued against whatever he publish'd, however uprightly design'd, and demonstratively true, whereas coming under the Disguise of a Third Person, as unconcern'd in the Matter, he met an impartial and candid Verdict ; viz. They could not see where the Dissenters were able to raise the least Exception, for that 'twas all clear Matter of Fact, what ought to have been considered at first ; and since they persevere to drive on at the same Jehu-rate, if it be not considered in due time, and that quickly too, they will drive all into Confusion.

And having thus pass'd the Pikes amongst his Friends, what those others say, or think, is the least of his Concern, having all along observ'd, how uneasie they are to be inform'd of any thing which tends to a Settlement, though amongst the rest, of their very selves : Opposing, and Pulling down, is the Delight of their Souls ; and if they cannot wreck their Spite upon the Church of England, and all that adhere to her, nothing shall continue in Peace, or rest in Quiet : For Confirmation whereof, take this Passage ; A Person of great Eminency, and very well acquainted with the Transactions of that Party, as well as most other Affairs, did lately, upon a Publick Occasion, declare that the Dissenters addres'd them-

selves

The Preface.

felves to the Deifts, thofe profefs'd Enemies of all Reveal'd Religion, (*and who abound too much in moſt great Poſts and Places*) to abett and countenance them in their Separation. *Whereas doubtleſs theſe Free-booters in Religion, if they be true Politicians, as they would by all means be thought, and muſt be fo, or nothing, will confider what* Dio Caſs. *tells us* Mecœnas *advis'd* Auguſtus, *upon his firſt Settlement of the* Roman Empire, That he ſhould follow conftantly the Religion eſtabliſh'd, for all Innovations therein tended to Sedition, and would fubvert his Government. *However the* Pious *Endeavours of thoſe others cannot ſurprize any one, who recollects what grateful* Acknowledgments *were made, when their good Friend Father* Petres *oblig'd them with a* Plenary Indulgence, *throwing all open by a* Difpenfing Power, *that the* Forfeitures *which thoſe of their* Lay-Brotherhood *incurr'd, by acting thereupon, ſhould never be taken notice of, when* Ways and Means *rack'd all the* Bufineſs-Wits *of the* Nation, *was a great* Favour *or great* Forgetfulneſs; *had any* Body *of* Churchmen *run themſelves into ſuch a* Premunire, *what a violent* Clamor *would it have made both within* Doors, and without? *But a* Fanatick *may ſteal the* Horfe *with more* Security, *than he after* Men *look over the* Hedge, *Although the forementioned* Addreſs *to the* Deifts, *if likely, might proceed from their more* Publick Difappointments, *in reference to this preſent* Parliament; *for as their early and earneſt* Solicitations *upon that account, were partly the occafion of this little* Tract; *according to what is therein hinted, fo hath it been ever ſince obſerv'd with how indefatigable an* Application *they endeavour'd to procure* Chofen Members *of their own* Pre-election; *tho', with no little* Satisfaction, *it ſhall be acknowledg'd their* Mifcarriages *and* Baffles *therein, hath abundantly exceeded* Expectation: *For in moſt* Counties *throughout the* Kingdom, *either they dar'd not to hazard the* Courfe, *or were ſhamefully outfaced if they did; neither met they with much better* Succeſs *in the feveral* Corporations *and* Burroughs, *Men by degrees are grown fo wise, at leaſtwiſe in their* Generation, *as to think it will turn to better account, if they chufe to ſerve themſelves, rather than a* Faction.

Yet notwithſtanding theſe, and many ſuch like vile Compliances, *with* Papifts, Deifts, Atheifts, *and what not? fo juſtly chargeable upon them, they can have the confidence ſtill to continue their old* Calumny *of* Popery *upon the* Church *of* England, *and every true* Member *thereof, unwilling to remember, though they cannot forget, with how difcreet a* Zeal, *and well manag'd* Refolution, *ſhe behav'd her ſelf in that* Critical Juncture, *when all the feveral* Sects *and* Factions, *ſneak'd like* Cowards, *or fomething worfe, not here to be nam'd. Upon which their unjuſt, and frontleſs* Freedom, *fome have thought it a little hard, that as the* Act *of* Indulgence *takes a great care, on the one hand, to ſecure the* Diſſenters *from the leaſt* Difturbance *or* Affront, *under a fevere* Penalty; *fo there ſhould be no* Provifion, *on the other, to reftrain them from bringing any* Charge *againſt the* Members, *or* Offices *of our* Church, *which they could not juſtifie: But wife* Men *would not attempt an* Impoſſibility, *knowing they might have as well enjoin'd an eternal* Silence *amongſt the* Females *at* Billingfgate. *The* Liberty *of their* Confciences *had been nothing without that of their* Tongues, *by which more eſpecially they think to prevail, and will have none to be* Lords *over them: Upon which* Charge *of the* Pſalmift *againſt* wicked Men, Pſal. 12. 4. *the* Learned *and* Pious Hammond *makes this* Paraphrafe: *Why ſhould we ſtand fo ſtrictly to confider, whether what we fay be true or no? So we may advantage our ſelves by it, to whom ſhould we be accountable for that?*

In fine, 'tis as natural for moſt of the feveral Separations *to bark at the* Church *of* England, *as a* Dog *at the* Moon, *and according to conjecture, for the fame reafon, they envy her* Splendor, *and* Prevention *of dark* Defigns, *which may* God *continue and advance, (for ſhe ſeems at preſent to be in the decreafe) and let them bark on till their* Throats *can hold out no longer; in hopes, nevertheleſs, our* World *may by degrees diſcover from what* Spirit *fuch* Railing Accufations *come; And the* Lord *in his due time* Rebuke *them.* Amen.

Octob. 14th
1698.

— M — N —

DUTCH *Way of* Toleration,

Moſt proper for our

ENGLISH DISSENTERS.

S I R,

THis returns my Thanks, for the Favour of your laſt, and *candid* Acknowledgment, that I had reaſon in affirming, " the *Sword* would continue to halt it on be- " tween St. *Paul*'s and *Pinner's-Hall*, as long as this Man " was *Mayor*; for now you were come over to my Opinion, " and ſaw it would not only be ſo, but that his *Succeſſor*, finding " the *Ice* thus broken, would, probably, follow in the ſame *Track*, " or otherwiſe improve the Affront to our old *Eſtabliſhments*, ac- " cording as the ſeveral *Factions*, which plac'd him in the *Chair*, ſhould " think fit to direct: Hereupon you deſire me to communicate what " I know in reference to the *Dutch Toleration*, (whereof you have " heard ſeveral hints in our private Converſe) and how it comes " to paſs, that the many *differing Perſwaſions* amongſt them, enjoy " their *Liberty* with a continued *Peace* and *Quiet*, whereas ours are " always *reſtleſs* and *encroaching*, every day graſping at more, and " ſeem ſtill diſſatisfied unleſs they can *engroſs* all.

Indeed, Sir, it was to my no little ſurprize, when laſt in Town, to find your ſelf, and ſome other Friends, ſo poſitive, that a *Re-primand* from the *Court of Aldermen*, and ſome by-*Reflections* in an Higher *Court*, would ſtifle their Deſign, or make them give it over, which I perceived was deeper laid, and had greater *Encouragements*, than any of you did then imagine; yet ſure this you muſt have ob-

ſerv'd

ferv'd, that 'tis very rare to find thofe *Parties* doing their bufinefs
by halves ; whatever *Lights* they may pretend to, there is an infal-
lible Argument to prove them *Children of this World*, being fo *wife*,
that is, *cunning*, in their *Generations*. No People carry on their
Projects with greater *Intrigue*, nor more nicely obferve the feveral
fteps and *degrees* by which they muft be accomplifhed : Their *Legal
Indulgence*, as it was a great Point gain'd, fo the timing of it was
very *critical* ; for, being in the heat of the *Revolution*, there might
be feveral. *Cafus omiffi*, which upon farther Debate would have
been better confidered ; particularly, I queftion very much, whether any *Diffenter* would have been allow'd going to the *Conventicle* during his *Magiftracy*, efpecially to carry the *Infignia* thither ;
the former of which hath been all along practis'd in feveral *Corporations* throughout the Kingdom ; and, doubtlefs, the *Prefident*
your *Lord Mayor* has fet, will be *Ap'd* by feveral of his *Brethren*
in other Places : (notwithftanding, as the Act runs at prefent, 'tis
a *Moot Cafe* among the Gentlemen of the *Long Robe*, whether al-
lowable thereby) But that your *Lord Mayor* may not have the
fole *Honour* of the firft Attempt, at leaft, that was done the Firft
Year of their *Indulgence*, at a *Corporation* in my Neighbourhood,
where an old *Zealot* of the 41 *Caufe* (brought in perhaps for that
purpofe) would needs have the *Mace* attend him to the *Barn* ; but
the honefty, or as they term'd it, obftinacy of the *Officers*, the
Serjeants, would not comply, and fo he went without it. After-
wards, indeed, when one of the fame Stamp was in courfe to be
chofen, the *Company* capitulated, that however the *Mayor* might
take his liberty, the *Mace* would be confin'd to *Church* ; which fome
though a little hard on the *Mace's* fide, fince 'twas believ'd every
whit as *tender-confcienc'd* as the Man who follow'd it.

But, to return to our purpofe, you fee how their Affairs ftand
at prefent, and how little they fcruple ftretching to the utmoft any
Liberty which is indulg'd them, whereof now they have a fair
Profpect to make a greater enlargement ; for you know next Win-
ter a New *Parliament* will come in courfe ; and they are fo far from
being *ignorant* thereof, or *idle* thereupon, as 'tis hard for a Perfon
of your *undefigning Integrity*, to imagine how earneftly they already
ftickle to carry on their Point in that *Critical Juncture*, *leave never
a Stone unturn'd*, are tampering with all *Interefts*, and in all *Places*,
to get confiding Members chofen, fuch *Root* and *Branch*-men, as
fhall effectually carry on *the Work of the Lord*, and once more eftablifh the *Good Old Caufe* ; and then let the *State* look to it as well
as the *Church*, for 'tis hard to refolve whether fuffer'd moft from

fuch

(3)

such *thorough Reformers*. Now this to me is Demonstration, that a *Religious Liberty*, a *Freedom* as to their *Consciences*, is not the sole, nor main thing they aim at; for then would they press no farther, that being confirm'd to them by *Legal Establishment*, to all Intents and Purposes imaginable: But to be dabbling in the *Government*, is as natural to them as *Water* to a *Fish*; and if they may not command the *Royalty*, and controul at Pleasure, prescribe who are *worthy Men*, and *Men worthy*, those Waters will be always troubled, never free from *foul Weather*, and *Storms*: Nay, farther to remark, how scandalously they prostitute their *Spiritual Liberty*, their *Right* of *Conscience*, to obtrude themselves upon the *Temporal* Power, their double dealing, playing *fast* and *loose* with our *Church* and *Sacrament*, is an irrefragable Argument. Formerly, the *Church* of *England* (to use their great *Patriarch's J. O's* Words) *was a meer Antichristian Encroachment upon the Inheritance of Christ, all her Darling-Errors, Stones of the* Old *Babel ; and therefore by no means to be communicated with : The Faithful of the Lord must not touch such defiled Garments ;* and this indeed was the common *Cant* of them all, for some score of Years together: Yet now we see, to serve a *State*-turn, or rather *overturn the State*, the Holy *Sacrament* goes down as glib with them, as the *Covenant* of old ; there is no *Scruple*, when the *Cause* is concern'd: In the mean while, I dare engage, that if this next *Election*, they can make a Party prevalent enough to repeal the *Test*, as they have already cancell'd the other *Penal Laws*, they will return to their *Old Invectives*, Our *Sacrament* shall be *Reprobated as an Antichristian Rite, and all Communion with our Church sinful and abominable.* Now here, if they would give me leave to expostulate a little, I would desire them to consider, whether any thing can bring a greater reproach upon *Religion*, the *Innocence*, and *Simplicity* of the *Gospel*, than such vain *Tergiversations* as these? Such *Linsy Woolsy Consciences :* Such *profane Halters between* God *and* Baal? Can we imagine there should be any thing more in all there *Mockeries*, than a *sordid Interest*, *spiteful Revenge*, or *popular Humour* ? To be cry'd up by the Factions, and make something of a Figure amongst the *Mob-Sectrries*, which they despair'd of obtaining from Men of *Sense* and *Principles*. This indeed is not exactly the *Laodicean* Temper; but the little difference is for the worse, being so *hot*, where they need not be so much as *lukewarm*, and less than so, where they should express a *religious Fervour* : And since *Almighty* God threatened to *spem the former out of his Mouth*, I fear his Blessings may be the less, if these others be not *spew'd out of the Government*.

B 2

And

And this, Sir, brings me to the *Queſtion* you propounded ; (and
what I preſume was chiefly aim'd at in the Acknowledgment you
made) *How it comes to paſs the* Dutch *live in ſo much Peace and Quiet,
notwithſtanding the many Perſwaſions tolerated amongſt them ?* Which
may be clearly anſwered in very few Words ; *viz. becauſe no ſuch
troubleſome, uneaſie People, as aforementioned, have to do in the Government.* And I have ſometimes admired our great Sticklers for *Liberty,* and *Toleration,* who upon all occaſions are too forward in
crying up the *Low-Country Model,* and pretending to be of a much
quicker Scent than others, never *hit off* this ; but, upon ſecond
Thoughts conſidered, they generally belong to ſome of the *Factions,*
and would be ſure not to exclude themſelves : Yet, doubtleſs, what
Horace obſerves in *Poetry,* is as true in *Politicks, Decipit exemplar
vitiis imitabile,* 'tis hard coming at the ſame end, without the like
means ; to imitate their *Toleration ,* without their *Caution* and
Reſtrictions, will not only be *ſordid,* as the Poet terms it, but *in-
effectual,* prove a *Remedy* worſe than the *Diſeaſe* ; for from thence,
more eſpecially, it proceeds, that their *Toleration* has turn'd to
Account : In all other Places, where *Univerſal and Unlimited,* it has
fallen a Prey to the undermining Stratagems of that *Spiritual Uſur-
per* upon all *Chriſtian Liberty* whatſoever, as will hereafter appear.
For your fuller ſatisfaction therefore, I ſhall give you an Account
of the *Dutch Toleration* ; as likewiſe how hard it will be to bring
us to that *Model,* and yet ſhew you 'tis that alone can do our bu-
ſineſs ; all other *Courſes* will be much more *unpracticable,* and *un-
ſafe,* and multiply thoſe *Diſtractions* which we deſign'd to prevent.
And that you may give the greater Credit to what I ſhall ſay herein,
it ſhall not depend upon my ſole *Authority* (though it was my chief
Enquiry during ſome Years abode there) but have the Confirmation of Sir *William Temple's Obſervations* upon thoſe *Provinces ;*
which, as I think it was the firſt, ſo 'tis, generally believed, the
exacteſt Piece we have had from that *Ingenious Gentleman ;* Clear
Matter of Fact, without that partiality and by-reſpect, which many times is not avoided by ſuch as pretend moſt thereunto.

Now what makes it ſeem more difficult and unpracticable a-
mong us, than them, is, That the *Conſtitution of their Government,*
and *Temper of their People,* will be found better adapted thereunto,
with ſome other Advantages of leſſer Moment ; All which take, as
follows.

Firſt, Then the *Conſtitution of Their Government* ſeems better
adapted thereunto : To which purpoſe, I muſt let you know, that
however thoſe *Provinces* are given out to be a *Common-Wealth,* a
Free

Free State, with such other swelling *Titles* of *Liberty*, *Priviledges*,&c. as if the People had the sole *Controll*, the *Dernier Refort*, in all *Publick* Determinations, (and so indeed it was in those little *Democracies* of *Greece*, and that great one of *Rome*, where no Laws could be enacted, nor *Magistrates* chosen, &c. but by their Consent) upon Enquiry it will appear quite otherwise; the *Populace*, the *Burghers*, have no more to do in the Government, than you and I, if we dwelt, or but sojourn'd amongst them: 'Tis the exactest *Oligarchy* that is this day, or perhaps ever was in the World, where the *Magistrates* of every *City*, or *Province*, are as absolute as any *Prince* in *Christendom*: Enact Laws, levy Taxes, chuse one another into the several Offices of *Government*, and upon a *Vacancy* (which seldom happens, but by death) elect another to fill up their number, without any controll, but from their *Stadtholder*, who hath a negative Voice, or somewhat like it in all their *Elections*; and though a reasonable Check, is what their *Hogan Moganships* have been most uneasie under, and endeavoured more than once to *free* themselves from. Sir *W. T.* instances more particularly in the City of *Amsterdam*, as chief of the *Province* of *Holland*, and in that, as chief of *Obs.* p. 97. the *Seven Provinces*; " and tells you, the *Government* of that *City* is " in the sole management of *Thirty six Persons*, whom he calls *Senators*; and saith, indeed, they were formerly chosen by the Voices " of the *Richer Burghers*, or *Feeemen* of the *City*; who, upon the " death of a *Senator*, met together either in a *Church*, a *Market*, or " some other Place, spacious enough to receive their Numbers, " and there made an *Election* of the Person to succeed, by a *Majority* of *Voices*. But about One hundred and thirty, or forty " Years ago, when the *Towns* of *Holland* began to encrease in " Circuit and People, so as these frequent Assemblies grew into " danger of *Tumult* and *Disorders*, upon every occasion, by reason " of their *Number* and *Contentions*; this *Election* of *Senators*, came " by the *Resolution* of the *Burghers* in one of their General *Assemblies*, to be devolv'd for ever upon the standing *Senate* for that " time; so that ever since when any of their Number dies, a new " one is chosen by the rest of the *Senate*, without any interven- " tion of the other Burghers, which makes the *Government* a sort of " *Oligarchy*, and very different from a *popular Government*, as it " is generally esteemed by those, who passing, or living in these " Countries, content themselves with common Observations, or " Inquiries. And this *Resolution* of the *Burghers* either was agreed " upon, or followed, by General Consent, or Example, about " the same time, in all the Towns of the *Provinces*, tho' with

" difference in the Number of the *Senators*. Thus far the foi emen-
tioned *Gentleman* ; whereto I muſt farther add, that theſe *Sena-*
tors both here, and in all other *Towns*, are of the ſame *Communion*,
as to the *Publick* Exerciſe of *Religion* ; which, after ſome Debates,
and Alterations, upon their *Defection* from *Spain*, was fix'd upon
the *Geneva*-Model, with an Allay of *Eraſtianiſm*, the better to
keep under the Inſolency of their *Presbyteries*, ſo troubleſome elſe-
where. 'Tis not of much moment to tell you farther, that as theſe
Senators marry generally into one anothers *Families*, ſo they keep
the *Government*, for the moſt part, amongſt themſelves, the *Chil-*
dren, with other *Relations*, coming in, and gradually aſcending, if
capable of it ; which nevertheleſs being faithfully diſcharg'd, without *Partiality*, *Avarice*, or any other ſuch by-reſpects, the People
ſeem no ways diſſatisfied therewith.

This, Sir, is a ſmall *Scratch* of the Preſent Eſtabliſhment of that
People, which I ſhall farther confirm to you, upon the Authority
of the preſent *Biſhop* of *Sarum* ; who, ſpeaking of the *Low Coun-*
tries, how they got their *Liberty*, and how they maintain'd it, adds,
yet after all this, though the Name of their Government has a greater
found towards Liberty than our own, we are really the much freer Peo-
ple of the two, where every Man has a more open acceſs to a proportion'd
Share in the Government, than among them.

The high-flown *Demagogues* of our *Nation*, I know, will cenſure
this as a great defect, a giving up their *Rights*, a betraying their
Priviledges, with a great deal ſuch like *Commonwealth-Cant*, as has
betray'd us into confuſion more than once ; whereas doubtleſs thoſe
thoughtful People made a ſober Judgment of Things, and well
underſtood ſuch *Priviledges* not worth keeping, as tended only to
the diſtraction of their *Debates*, and might, in the end, deſtroy
their *Government :* To be ſure the General *Toleration*, which followed ſoon after, could have ſtood upon no other *Bottom* ; and
thoſe at the *Helm* were ſo well ſatisfy'd, with this New *Conſtitution*,
as to ſet the *Sovereignty* of all the *Seven Provinces* upon the ſame
Foot: For ſo the *Aſſembly of the States General, which conſiſted of a-*
bove Eight hundred Perſons, who meeting together in one Place from ſo
many ſeveral Parts, gave too great a ſhock to the whole Body of the
Union, made their Debates long, and ſometimes confuſed, the Reſolutions
ſlow, and upon ſudden Occaſions out of time, was by mutual Conſent of the
whole Body, devolved upon thoſe, now ſtil'd the States General, which
conſiſts of ſo many Deputies from each Province, more or leſs, as they
are pleaſed to ſend ; which makes no difference, as to their Votes, be-
cauſe given according to their ſeveral Provinces, not number of
Perſons,

Peace and
Union. p. 9.

Sir W. T.
p. 110.

Perfons, although their number feldom arife to fo many as the *Senate* at *Amfterdam* confifts of.

Now, Sir, to come to the *difparity*, in reference to our felves, none of this is done, or muft be thought of amongft us, as to the whole *Body* of the *Government*; which, though a *Free Monarchy*, is fo well temper'd, as we fee every *Subject* own'd to have more *Liberty*, than under a *Free State* : 'Tis pity it fhould be fo much abufed; yet fince it is fo, might not there be fome *Abridgment* as to particular Perfons, without the leaft Infraction upon the whole Conftitution, an Exchange of *Temporal* for a *Spiritual Liberty*? They that will have a New *Religion*, let them live according to this New *Model* of our *Neighbours*, and forbear meddling in *Civil* Concerns; otherwife I cannot fee how the *Old Eftablifhment* fhould be long upheld : For whilft the *Tolerated Parties* are free to *Vote*, and put in their Claims to all *Publick Adminiftrations*, all *Offices* of *Honour*, *Truft*, or *Profit*, they may carry things as they pleafe; what thorough their *Induftry* and *Importunity*, *Cabals* and *Clamours*, *Libels* and *Lies*, 'tis as poffible to ftop a raging Sea, as the Madnefs of fuch People; No Man of Sence will attempt it; for tho' they are divided amongft themfelves, in *Doctrines*, *Modes of Worfhip*, and *Forms of Government*, *Ephraim* againft *Manaffeh*, and *Manaffeh* againft *Ephraim*; yet the *Judah* of the *Church* of *England*, is the united Object of all their Spites, and what they ftudy moft implacably to fupplant and deftroy : And if we reflect how many of them, in the late Reign, comply'd with the *Difpenfing* Power, and fuperfeded all thofe Laws which the Nation, for above an hundred Years fucceffively, had compil'd to fecure the *Proteftant Religion*, there needs no Window into any of their Breafts, (as a leading . *Holder-Forth* then wifh'd in an *Addrefs*) to difcover the *Reality of their Intentions*, 'tis too clear from thence, and all their other Practices, that the *Church of England* is the only *Popery* they have a Pique againft; and can confederate with that which is really fo; nay, *Turk* or *Jew*, to effect its Ruine. In my Judgment, therefore, It would be a very reafonable, and neceffary *Teft*, (and, I fancy, reduce the truly confcious *Diffenters* to a very fmall number) to try the fincerity of their *Intentions*, and fteadinefs of their *Principles*, by an *Indulgence* of that *Liberty* they are fo zealous for, upon Condition not to intermeddle in *Civil Affairs*, which their weak *Underftandings*, ftrong *Prejudices*, and vain *Enthufiafms*, render them moft unqualified for : Will the *Freeholder*, even to the *Cottager*, with his *Cabbage*-ground and *Apple-Tree*, recede from the Right he has of throwing up his *Cap* at a *Country-Election*? The Members of fmaller

ler *Burroughs*, as well as larger *Corporations*, of putting their *Bur-*
geſſes to an Expence upon the like account, together with· beiŋg
on the *Livery*, ſtrutting at *Common Halls*, *Common Councils*, and
the like ? Nay, even in Country-Parriſhes, will they recede from
ſerving as *Conſtable* in their turns, controling the Poor as Over-
ſeers, or *Parſons* as *Church-Wardens* ? So likewiſe the *Country-Gen-*
tleman ; how will he take being left out of the *Peace*, or not ap-
pearing upon the *Bench* at *Seſſions*, and *Aſſizes*, as well as his Con-
forming *Neighbours* ?· If I miſtake not the Temper of the ſeveral
Parties, theſe little things will be of hard digeſtion, ſince they have
been ever obſerv'd as forward to *Command*, as uneaſie to *Obey* ; yet
if we would go according to the *Low-Country-Plan*, (to uſe the
New Word) this courſe muſt be taken ;· for 'tis this alone has ſe-
cur'd them, and this, or nothing, will ſecure us : And therefore
a very *learned Perſon*, about Eighteen or Twenty Years ſince, who
underſtood the *Unreaſonableneſs* of our ſeveral *Separations* extreme-
ly well, had fully ſtudied all their Cavils, and as fully evinced
them, if any thing of *Eviction* could work upon that ſort of People :

Pref. p.85. Yet, in his Preface to that *Demonſtrative* Piece, whether it was to
let the *Diſſenters* ſee, he was averſe to nothing which might tend
to a *Settlement*, or propounded it from a Friend, whoſe Head hath
been always pregnant with *Comprehenſion*, and *Toleration-Projects :*
Or, perhaps, to humour ſome great Men at the *Helm*, who about
that time ſtickled very much for a *Suſpenſion* of *Penal Laws* ; upon
what Deſign, as every Eye then diſcover'd, ſo, I fear, in ſpite of
all Endeavours to the contrary, that Deſign will be ever concern'd
therein, and advanc'd thereby.; I ſay, upon whatever Account it
was, this *Reverend Worthy* Perſon, in his *Preface*, makes a ſhort
Eſſay as to a *Toleration*, laying down ſuch *Reſtrictions* and *Limitations*,
as are requiſite to prevent the Miſchiefs of an unlimited *Licentiouſ-*
neſs, which, he ſaith, *would certainly bring Confuſion amongſt us, and in*
the end, Popery : Now the firſt of his *Reſtrictions*, is, *That none be*
permitted this Indulgence, who do not declare, that they hold all Commu-
nion with our Church unlawful ; for it ſeems unreaſonable to allow it to
others, and will give countenance to endleſs and cauſeleſs Separations.
And give me leave to add, will gratifie the *Capricio's* of ſuch wan-
ton Libertines, as live *Scepticks*, and dye *Atheiſts :* To which kind
of *Scepticiſm* I find ſeveral, who aſſociate with, at leaſt, and abett,
the *Diſſenters*, much inclin'd, *Quere*, as to your Lord M----   Another *Reſtriction* is, *That no Perſon, ſo indulg'd, be capable of any Pub-*
lick Office ; it being unreaſonable, that ſuch ſhould be truſted with Govern-
ment, who look upon what the Government hath already eſtabliſh'd, as un-
wawfull.

lawful: A Third is, *That all such as enjoy it, must declare the particular Congregation they are of; and enter their Names before such Commissioners as shall be authoriz'd to that purpose.* I shall mention no more, (tho' there be several others tending to the same purpose) but only appeal whether you, or any Man else of sober Sence, must not acknowledge these to be highly reasonable, and absolutely necessary, that we may know what *Men* are, and where to have them. In *Martial Law*, none are more severely proceeded against, than such as fly from their own, or are taken as *Spies* in the Enemies *Camp* ; yet we must suffer these Enemies of our Church, tho' they have been all along in the *Dissenters* Service, to enter our Line at pleasure, take our *Word*, our *Test*, and *Sacrament*, that they may be the better qualified to work our Ruine ; nay, are so stupidly senceless, as not only to let them alone, but entertain and caress them as Friends : Just thus the *Amalakites* serv'd *Israel*, and we know how highly Almighty *God* was incensed thereat, and what the People suffer'd thereby. But not to ramble too far, or be thought too much concern'd upon the *Church*-Account, let us consider our *Government* in General, whether it can be so well secur'd by such an *Hodge-podge* of Perswasions, who will be continually pulling several ways, and aiming at several Interests? As the *Low Countries*, where a few understanding Men, *Act* unanimously for the *Publick Welfare*, without any by-Regards, or *Factious Designs*.

Secondly, What I mentioned, in the next place, by way of *Disparity*, as likely to make a *Toleration* less feasable amongst us, than the *Dutch*, is the *different Temper* and *Humours* of the Two Nations : They are a *serious*, and *thoughtful* People, wholly intent upon their own private Concerns, and very industrious in all their particular *Callings* ; frugal and parsimonious to the utmost ; truly speaking, necessitated thereunto, by reason of the many and continual *Imposts* laid upon them, which no People under Heaven so contentedly bear, nor so indefatigably wade through, being abundantly satisfied with the *Prudence* and *Integrity* of their *Governours*, and highly transported with an imaginary Conceit of *Liberty*, which no body can see into, or understand, but themselves : So that, as the forementioned *Gentleman* observes, *All Appetites and Passions seem to run lower here, than in other Countries.* I am sure they do not run so low in ours, which, on the contrary, is too *sanguine* to be settled as it ought ; for, to pass by that old Charge of *Rex Diabolorum*, the *English good Nature* was so strangly sowr'd by our late Times of *Libertinism*, and *Confusion*, Men contracted such a habit of *Self-conceit*, *Opposition*, and *Disobedience*, were so totally given

C

o er

over to a perverse *Enthusiastical* Spirit ; and for so long a time, as now indeed it may be look'd upon, next to impossible, absolutely to *conjure* it down ; yet doubtless it ought to be confin'd to its own home, the *melancholy Tombs* of their restless unquiet Thoughts, and not wander up and down the World, to possess others with the *Legions* of such *Frenzies*; which, if let alone, will certainly be; for 'tis a *Pestilent* Infection, and without due Caution spreads like the *Plague.* And that this unhappy Disposition began from the *Separation-Fraternity*, and is much more incident to the *English*, than *Dutch* Temper, take this single *Instance :* There were more *Disputes*, *Contests*, and *Quarrels*, amongst the few *Brownists*, and other *Independant Sectaries*, which resorted thither the latter end of Queen *Elizabeth*'s, King *James* the First's time, and so on, than among the whole *Dutch* Nation ever since they *Reform'd*: 'Tis unaccountable what impertinent *Controversies* arose between them, even to the Colour of *Aaron*'s *Ephod*, whether it were *Blew*, or a *Sea-green*, which made an irreconcilable difference between their *Pastors*, and consequently the *Flocks* divided.

Once indeed there was a *Controversie* amongst the *Dutch*, about some *School*-Points, (and I think that the only Instance can be given) which rose to a great height ; but then you must know it was occasioned principally by two great *State-Factions*, wherein most *Divines*, especially of the *Geneva*-Cut, are too easily made *Properties :* In this, to be sure, they serv'd themselves to purpose ; for obtaining by *Power*, what they could not get by *Argument*, one Party became *Judge* of the other, and thrust them down amongst the several *Herds* of *Tolerated Dissenters.* And here give me leave to observe a farther Evidence of the peaceable Temper and Disposition of those People; for tho' the *ablest*, and most *learned* in their *Government*, have all along laugh'd at the *Stoical Fatality*, and *Reprobation-Rigours* of their Divines, and know what hard measure the *Remonstrants* the *Arminians* had met withal; yet never thought it worth while to have the Debate reviv'd, which might only revive new *Exasperations* about insignificant *Opinions*; or, as I find it express'd in a late Poem, *for Points by neither Party understood.* On the other side, to return home, how differently have these Disputes been manag'd amongst us, and how vexatiously continued ? *Arminian and Papist*, pass'd a long time for Terms *synonimous*; which not only the *Pulpit-Beautifeus*, but several *Grandees* of the *House*, maliciously apply'd to every *Orthodox Divine*, and indeed all others, who would not go along with them in those cursed *Desolations* they then brought upon *Church* and *State*; which having

wretchedly

wretchedly effected, how did the *Religious Brawl* multiply upon their Hands? With what implacable Enmity, did the *Presbyterian* and *Independant* profecute each other? And how violent in their feveral ways, both againſt them, and one another, were the numerous Spawn of *Equivocal Sects*, which like the overflowing *Nile*, their *Deluge* of Miſchiefs ſo fatally produc'd? Inſomuch, as when *Cromwel* had beſtrid the *Commonwealth*, and ſet himſelf in the *Saddle*, he was preſum'd to connive at feveral *Church of England* *Congregations*, both in *Publick Pariſhes*, and *Private Aſſemblies*, in ſpite to the *Presbyterians*, and other *Sectaries*, whom he dreaded as much as the *Loyal Party*; and did, with reaſon, expect they ſhould improve thoſe *Calumnies*, and *Invectives* againſt him, whereof he had been the grand Promoter againſt their *Rightful*, and *Lawful King*; and ſo he found it to his End, which that perplexity and vexation he met with from *Fanaticks* of all ſorts, and in all Places, *City*, *Country*, but eſpecially his *Army*, was preſum'd to haſten.

'Tis true, when the *Legiſlative* Power, the other day, thought fit to *eſtabliſh* them an *Indulgence*, there was a Project ſet on-foot to make *Two Sticks* one, (to uſe their own *Canting Terms*) and feveral Propoſals laid down in order thereunto; yet we find them ſtill ſeparated from one another, and the feveral Parties, upon every little occaſion, dividing among themſelves, tho' much Art is uſed to ſmother and conceal it: At the beſt, it was but a Flouriſh, a *Cord of Vanity*, which bound them together, and it held accordingly; neither can you expect otherwiſe, upon conſideration of the *Cauſes* which that great *Undertaker* aſſigns of thoſe *Diviſions*, the *Root from whence their Diſcords ſpring: Come they not hence, even* **Two Sticks** *of our Luſts? Whatever you find to have been the Cauſe of them, whe-* **made one,** *ther Spiritual Pride, or a Contentious Diſpoſition, or an Affectation of* **p. 28.** *Singularity, or Error of Opinion, or Admiration of Mens Perſons, or a Sowrneſs of Spirit, or an Ambition of drawing Diſciples after us: Let the Cauſe be what it will, it muſt be remov'd,* &c. All which is ſooner ſaid then done; ſuch *Pecadillo's*, and of ſo long Continuance, are not eaſily diſlodg'd: Although he might as well have taken his *Character* from *St. Paul's Perilous Times*, which he foretells **2 Tim. 3.** in the laſt Days, when Men ſhould be *Heady*, *High-minded*, *Covet-* **Ver. 9.** *tous*, *Proud*, *Boaſters*, &c. ſo far from growing better, as he declares they ſhould *wax worſe and worſe*, *deceiving*, *and being deceived*. Now, *Sir*, whatever Cenſure I may incur from others, my Appeal is to your ſelf, whether the Account here given of theſe People be any other, than what their daily Practices do ſadly verifie?

fie? And if left to their own *Culture*, and *Ingenuity*, any likelihood they should reform? 'Tis grown as cuftomary, as habitual with them, to *thwart*, *contradict*, and *oppofe*, as with the *Dutch* to *live quietly*, and *mind their own bufinefs* : From which Difpofition of theirs, I may continue the Difparity, and obferve,

Thirdly, How their conftant *application* to Bufinefs and Imployment, afford them no time to *dream* of *New Lights*, or trouble themfelves about any other Perfwafion, as to *Religion*, than what they were brought up in: For, as at their firft *Eftablifhment*, there were *Three* predominant Ways of Opinion, (I won't fay Doctrine) and Worfhip, which they had then Reform'd themfelves into, *Lutherans*, *Calvinifts*, and *Anabaptifts* ; fo the *Toleration* more efpecially extended to them, and has been generally continued down in the fame Families, from *Father* to *Children*, ever fince; neither is it fo ufual with them to *flitt up and down*, from one *Maggotty Perfwafion* to another, as amongft us. Thofe upftart puny. Sects, which arofe of later Days, are moftly Foreign, and moftly from *England* too, as the *Brownifts*, and *Independants* firft, the *Sabbatarians* after them, then *Quakers*, *Muggletonians*, and what not? Who have prevail'd with fome of the Natives to be as foolifh and mad as themfelves, but not many ; and, perhaps, had they been kept to the fame Thoughtfulnefs at home for Bread, and all other Neceffaries of Life, would not fo wantonly have gone *a-Whoring with their own Inventions.*

And the like reafon may be given, that there are not fo many *Libertines*, *Atheiftical*, *Profane Perfons*, as in many other Parts, where all *Religions* are *Tolerated* : It cannot feem ftrange there fhould be fome without any; and that there are not more, fhall not be attributed fo much to their *Vertue* as *Neceffity* ; for not only their *Mechanicks* and *Tradefmen*, but Perfons of the beft *Quality*, are oblig'd to the like Care and Induftry, as to the Concerns of Humane Life. The Ground on which their many populous Cities ftand, is of fmall Compafs ; and the *Rents* of that little *Land* they have, are very low, not able to maintain any one in the Port of a *Gentleman*, (that is, an *Idleman*, which is their Term for that degree) whereof as there are few *Ancient Families* amongft them, fo the Children of thofe that are, as likewife of their *Chief Magiftrates*, and *Rich Merchants*, are conftantly brought up to fome *Imployment*, *Military* or *Civil*, with an *Education* agreeable thereunto, which, together with their Natural Difpofition, keeps their Thoughts *fix'd* upon things really *advantageous* ; and fo you fhall generally find them very *intent* upon their *Defigns*, and *affiduous* in in their *Application*. Will you give me leave to apply this, and obferve how oppofite their Courfe is to that of our *Mercurial Wits*, who being born to great *Fortunes*, and valued for the great Worth of thofe *Predeceffors* which rais'd them, as if nothing elfe were wanting which fhould recommend them to the World, think themfelves above any ferious *Application*, either as to Bufinefs, or Knowledge. I need not tell you how little, or no, *Education* our young *Mafter* has from his very Cradle; how careful the good *Lady-Mother* is, he fhould not be kept in too much at *School* ; what a fruitlefs Figure he makes in the *Univerfity*; and when he comes up to the *Extravagancies* of the Town, is as much for living a-bove *fober Sence*, as our *Diffenters* above *Ordinances*. God forbid this fhould be a *General Rule* ; yet it could be wifh'd there were more *Exceptions*, than daily Experience will permit us to obferve : *Liberty of Life*, tho' not fo much clamour'd for, is as much in Vogue as *Liberty of Confcience*, and the one doubtlefs confequent of the other : For the practical *Atheift* hath been ever thought to intro-duce the *Speculation*; and when Men are left free to all *Religions*, that is the proper time to fet up for none. I remember, during Cromwel's *Ufurpation*, the *Leviathan-Doctrine* was firft ftarted ; and as fome *Gentlemen* of too good Parts, unlefs better employ'd, were induftrious to cultivate and improve it, fo many of our *Airy Sparks* about *Town*, and elfewhere, became their *fordid Imitators* : Nothing would go down with them, but a *State of War*, with a total Abolition of all *difference between Good and Evil, Right and Wrong*. Now, whether it was their being *uneafy*, or *afham'd*, of-fuch unreafonable *Notions*, or an affectation of *Novelty*, the delight of *vain Minds*, *Deifm* feems to have fuperfeded that, and is be-come at prefent the Darling-Subject of every young *Libertine's* Dif-courfe ; who will prefume to expofe, and run down *Reveal'd Religion* with all Confidence imaginable, altho' the little *Impertinent* never thought a fober hour in its life ; and underftands the *Philo-fophy* of *Matter* and *Motion*, no farther, than that his own *Brains* are in a *continual Hurry* : Not but that thefe *Engines* too are fet on work by fome more *plodding Heads*, who have feveral fecret De-figns in exploding the *Authority of Scripture*, upon the *Politick*, as well as *Prophane Account* ; and, among the reft, to *buy up* fuch *Models of Government*, as the *Belief* thereof exprefly *overthrows*. Here then arifes the main *Quere:* What fhall we do with fuch *Difputers* as thefe? The *Sceptick*, the *Deift*, the *Atheift*, under what *Clafs* fhall we place them? They have the fame *Plea* to be confider'd, which the others always brought, that is, *Number and Wealth*;

being

being able to vie, in either Particular, with any of their differing *Factions*, and, for ought I fee, in a fhort time, may outdo them all; fince daily Experience affures us 'tis the laft refult of *Fanatick Zeal*; for being *over-heated* and *weary*, with running its feveral *Courfes* of *Faction* and *Opinion*, it fits down in the end, and centres here. And yet, all this while, the reft will not fee what a fine Thread they have fpun for themfelves, as well as us; whilft the one are undermining the *Church* of *England*, thefe others are doing the fame to the *Chriftian Religion* : Altho', to fpeak impartially, the *Latitude* fome Divines have taken, as to the *Socinian*, and other Points of like Nature, muft be acknowledg'd not a little conducing to this Grand *Apoftacy* ; fo readily will *Corrupt Minds* improve bad *Principles*, deny thofe *Myfteries* by wholefale, which fome Mens *rafh* and *nice Enquiries* had made more perplex'd and intricate, than the *Simplicity* of True *Religion* ftands in need of. or did ever defign. And this, Sir, is the refult of an *Unlimited Toleration*; which going on at this rate, (unlefs the *Pater Nofter* Men interpofe their *Inquifition*) muft neceffarily end in a *Sit anima mea cum Philofophis.*

Fourthly, Another thing which makes the *Dutch Toleration* fit the more *eafie*, is, That Their *Government* is moft *exact* and *punctual* in the *Adminiftration* of *Juftice*, and *Execution* of *Laws*; which as they are *enacted* at firft, upon the mature deliberation of a few fober underftanding Men, with fole regard to the *Common Weal*, the *Publick Good*; fo, once *proclaim'd*, there is no avoiding their true *Import*, or efcaping the *Penalty* of a *Violation* : The *Lawyers* among them dare not *Open*, or fo much as *Quetch* againft what their Superiours have thought fit to *eftablifh*, much lefs ftudy *Flaws*, and *hammer out Niceties*, to gratifie Men, in fruftrating, whatever good the *Legiflative Power* defign'd, and put them to the trouble of an *Explanatory Act* next *Seffion*, which runs the fame rifque : Yet that we are under thefe very Circumftances, I need not tell you ; which, with the Infolency of *Faction*, the remiffnefs and indifferency of the *Executive Power*, hath brought us to too nigh an Affinity with that deplorable Eftate of the *Jewifh Anarchy*, *where every one did what feem'd right in his own eyes.* Otherwife, we have *Laws* more than enough ; and could they have executed themfelves, all Allegations for a *Toleration* had been long fince quafh'd ; not only the *Externals* of *God's Publick Worfhip* had been kept up in *Decency* and *Order*, but every Man's *Temporal* Concern, his *Right* and *Property*, fix'd upon a much furer *Bottom.* On the contrary, a *Licentioufnefs* and Indifferency, as to *Religious Duties*, hath fo far *unprincipled and*

and debauch'd Mens Minds, that our modern *Faith* is not only without *Works*, but fo wholly confin'd to fome *Spiritual Chimæra's*, as there is little of *Truth* or *Truft* in the ordinary Tranfactions of *Humane Life :* Our *Meum* and *Tuum* is in a very precarious Condition, what with the *Latitude* of their new Notions, and the advantage to be taken from the *Perplexity*, the *Niceties* of our *Laws*, with the little *Tricks* of Practice, fo fhamefully now-a-days *alla-mode*, an undefigning *Integrity* can fcarce tell whom to truft, and is frequently at a lofs, either to *recover Right*, or repel *Wrong :* Neither will it be ever otherwife, as long as fo many *Law-jobbing Make-bates* are fuffered to fwarm in every *County* throughout the *Kingdom*. Were *Grievances* to be *redrefs'd* by their Malignity and *epidemick* Contagion, I know no one thing fooner to be confider'd ; that it is otherwife, you and I cannot help. In fhort, Sir, that a *Strict* and *Regular Execution* of *Laws*, is the Life and Soul of any *Government*, take thefe two different Inftances : In the *Spanifh Netherlands*, we find the *Romifh Religion* folely eftablifh'd, with the *Rigour*, though not the Name, of that *Inquifition* ; which was the moft plaufible *Plea* for their firft *Defection :* On the other fide, in the *United Provinces*, there is a general *Toleration* ; both which, the *Uniformity* of the one, and *Indulgence* of the other, are fupported, and kept up, by a vigorous Execution of fuch *Laws* as are thought moft proper thereunto ; and if either, the latter are more exact and fevere, by reafon it is fo natural for different *Opinions* to *clafh* with, and *thwart* each other ; fo far are they from admitting them into the *Magiftracy*, giving the leaft way to *New Lights*, and *Fanciful Enthufiafms* there, as well knowing fuch a *Freedom* is enough to make any *Government* as *monftrous* as that *Picture*, which had an *Hinc Populus* affix'd.

Fifthly, I fhall only add farther, that the *Dutch Toleration* was eftablifh'd in the *Infancy* of the *Reformation*, when Men had a fincere and unfeigned *Zeal* for the Truth of Religion; defired nothing more than to have her *free'd* from *Ignorance* and *Superftition*, fuch fpurious *Doctrines*, and burthenfome *Ceremonies*, as ruft of Time, neglect of Enquiry, and, above all, the *Intrigues of Papal Ufurption*, had impos'd upon the World, and for feveral *Centuries* together made pafs for *Catholick*. Now, although this *Zeal* was not always *according to Knowledge*, the different, and, in fome Places, not juftifiable *Methods* which were taken, did much *obftruct*, ay, and *fcandalize* fo good an Undertaking ; yet the main Point being gain'd, in fhaking off the *Roman Yoke*, whether out of *Intereft*, *Prudence*, or *Piety*, I fhall not determine, Men generally fat down abundantly fatisfied

fatisfied with the Enjoyment of that Perfwafion, which made the deepeft Impreffion upon their *Minds :* And this happened in fuch a juncture for the *United Provinces,* as perhaps no Age will be ever able to *paralel* : For the *Spanifh Intereft* prevailing in *Brabant,* and *Flanders,* with the *Walloon Provinces,* whoever could, or would not fubmit, retreated hither, as likewife great multitudes out of *France* and *Germany* ; which made them the *Pantheon,* the common Receptacle of all People pretending to *Liberty of Confcience,* the only thing then defired, and in the enjoyment whereof (whether well or ill-inform'd, we are not now to enquire) they were abundantly fatisfied.

How much the World (efpecially amongft us) is *cool'd* as to fuch a *Temper,* and *heated* as to much worfe *Difpofitions,* our many *Feuds* and *Factions,* unreafonable *Cavils,* and implacacable *Enmities,* too fadly declare. Men now-a-days, bellow out the *Proteftant Religion,* the *Proteftant Religion,* as the *Jews* of old, *The Temple of the Lord, The Temple of the Lord,* as if the Name, or Relation thereunto, might Authorize the groffeft Impieties, their wilful *Perjuries,* and *Seditious* Practices, the Violation of *Publick Laws,*and *Difturbance* of *Publick Peace,* even to a moft unnatural *Rebellion,* and execrable *Regicide :* This, Sir, impartially fpeaking, is undeniable Matter of Fact ; and if ever the Nation returns to its *Wits* again, *fober Senfe,* and *found Principles,* fuch *Principles,* will be *recorded* with a very *black* Character, the Reproach not only of the *Reformation,* but of every thing which tends to true *Religion,* like *Pharaifees* and *Zealots* among the *Jews,* facrificing all to their own grofs *Hypocrifie,* fordid *Avarice,* and felf-will'd *Ambition* ; and God grant they do not bring the like *fatal End upon our Place and Nation* : The dreadful apprehenfion whereof makes not only my Hand, but my Heart tremble ; and, amidft fuch *melancholy* Reflections, wifh to have been born in an Age, when *Wife Men* had had the Afcendent of *Fools,* and *Honeft Men* of *Knaves :* On the contrary, as things now ftand, you know the Clofe of that Old *Rhime, Knaves and Fools will quite undo us.*

Neither can our Profpect be much better, if we look upon the *Reformation* abroad : What a ftrange Indifferency have fome *Great Princes* of the *Empire* lately difcover'd? And how grofs the *Apoftacy* of others? To be fure, where there was a *General Toleration* of *Lutheran* and *Calvinifts,* together, with the feveral other differing Perfwations, *Anabaptifts, Arrians, Socinians,* &c. they are either wholly extirpated, as in *Bohemia, Moravia,* the Two *Auftria's, Poland,* &c. or in a fair Tendency thereunto, as at prefent in

Hun-

Hungary, and *Tranfilvania* : In all which Places they were very nu-merous ; but what with contending amongſt themſelves, and *in-novating*, or *oppoſing* the *Eſtabliſh'd Government*, they have been ei-ther worm'd, or beaten out, with all the contempt and eaſe ima-ginable : And that the ſame Deſign is carrying on amongſt us, and the ſame Event expected, they muſt be wilfully blind who do not ſee, what with *Licentiouſneſs* on the one hand, and *Hypocriſie* on the other, the no-*Reality* of ſuch as pretend moſt, and great *Indiffe-rency* of all the reſt ; as we are naturally prone to fall into Extreams, ſo we ſeem ſtrangely diſpos'd (and the more, becauſe unwilling to believe it) to fall into that which we have all along pretended moſt vehemently to avoid.

Thus, Sir, have I *impartially*, and perhaps too *freely*, told you, what I know, and what I think of the *Dutch Toleration* ; yet with-out this *Freedom*, it had been impoſſible to ſet you in a *True Light*, ſo as to diſcover the groſs miſtakes of our *Commonwealth* Preten-ders who are always admiring the *Hollanders*, with the Excellent *Adminiſtration* People live under there ; which nevertheleſs they underſtand no more, than how the *Empire*, and *Army* of *Ruſſia*, is now manag'd during the *Czar*'s Abſence ; and the many *Projects* they are ſo troubleſome withal, both in *Theory and Practice*, are as op-poſite thereunto, as one *Pole* to the other : Yet, ſince things are brought to that paſs, as a *Toleration* muſt be, give me leave to tell you, that venturing in any other than a *Dutch* Bottom, will *ſhip-wreck* the whole *Cargo* ; that is, without a *Metaphor*, keeping the *Magiſtracy* in ſuch hands as ſhall be of one *Piece*, *Uniform*, and *Una-nimous* in the *Management* thereof ; for which I ſhall briefly lay down theſe following Reaſons, and ſo end your Trouble.

1ſt. We ſhall have ſome Face of *Government* in an *Eſtabliſh'd Na-tional Religion* ; which I mention ſolely upon a *Civil Account*, and that not only in regard to the outward *Decorum*, (which yet ought to be conſider'd) but the abſolute Neceſſity thereof, as the only means of preventing thoſe continual *Contraſts* and *Caballings*, which the ſeveral *Factions* will have one againſt another ; and if admitted to *Debates* , all together againſt that which is uppermoſt ; the Miſchief, and Inconveniencies whereof, can no other way be re-dreſs'd , than by fixing the *Ruling Power* in one Perſwaſion, to whom it ſhall ſolely appertain to take care of the whole, ſee the ſeveral *Parties* enjoy their private *Opinions*, without the leaſt Infra-ction upon our *Publick Peace*. On the other ſide, let us reflect, firſt, upon the *Undecency* of the thing, how prepoſterous it muſt ſeem to any Man of *Sence*, whether *Native* or *Forreigner*, that the *Sword*

D   ſhould

should dance attendance from one Place to another, according to the *Caprice* of each prevailing *Faction*: This Year's *Lord Mayor* has a *Conscience* of such *Latitude*, as to *Trim* it between *Church* and *Conventicle*, without the least regret ; whereas his *Successor* may have one so *squeamish*, and *streight-lac'd*, as not to come within the Sound of St. *Paul's Organ*, or under the roof of that *Sumptuous*, and therefore *Superstitious Structure*. But then too having got the *Sword* to go their own way, how strangely must it wander up and down; as each Party prevail to get into the *Chair* ; one Year it must attend a *Presbyterian*-Meeting, the next, perhaps, will fall to the *Independant* s Lot, and the *Anabaptists* will ill resent it to go without their turn ; nay, we are not sure but the *Quakers* may put in their Claim, and without any Offence to the *Inward-Man*, desire it should attend their *Motions* on a bulk in *Grace-church-street*. This, Sir, I take to be as *Natural* to the aspiring *Spirits* of those several *Schismatical Herds*, as *Milk* to a *Calf*, and they will *low* as much if kept without it ; yet how decent this will be, how unbecoming the *State* and *Gravity* of any *Magistracy*, I leave for you, and the World to judge. However that of *Publick Security* is much more to be consider'd ; for whatever *Pleas* may be alledg'd, or *Protestations* made, we know how things went, when the *weak Conscience* had got the *strongest Sword*, *Dominion was then founded in Grace*, and the appointed time come for the *Saints* to inherit the *Earth*, and bring in *Subjection all the Powers of Darkness*.

2dly, The *Ancient Grandeur and Hospitality* of our *City-Magistracy*, and proportionably of all other *Corporations*, will be hereby continued and kept up ; which since it came into these hands, hath been most *scandalously* slighted, and disus'd ; for the *Character* which our *Poet Laureat* gave of that cursed *Shimei*, who first led the Van to *Faction* and *Frugality*, is true of all the rest, *Cool are their Kitchens, tho' their Brains are hot.* To speak freely, a *sneaking*, *single-soul'd Sectary*, cannot exert it self to any thing that is *Great* or *Generous*, *Gain* is their *Godliness*, and *Profit* their *Preferment* ; in order whereunto, upon Enquiry, you shall find, that those *Great Offices* wherein worthy *Citizens* were formerly wont to expend several thousand Pounds, are now made to bear their own Charges, and bring somewhat into Pocket too: And, as a farther ill consequence hereof, there are those will tell you all *Places of Inferiour Trust* are dispos'd off accordingly ; and whoever makes a hard *Bargain*, will be more *solicitous* for his own *Reimbursement*, than the *Commonweal*. 'Twas nobly said of *Tully*, *Nec quidquam aliud videndum est nobis, quos Populus Romanus hoc in Gradu collocarit, nisi ne quid*

quid privatis ſtudiis de operâ publicâ detrahamus ; neither can it poſſi-
bly go. well with any *Government*, if Men in *Publick Places* have not
Publick Spirits, under which defeſt I am afraid our poor *Nation*, at
preſent more eſpecially, very much *labours*.

  3*dly*, This will make an exaſt *Diſcrimination* between the truly
conſcientious Diſſenter, and the *Politick*, the *Factious Intriguer* ; for
when every Man muſt declare to what *Body* of *Church-Memberſhip*
he will *join*, and is oblig'd therein to abide, (whether in the *Lord*, or
not, the ſame *Lord* ſhall judge at laſt) our ſundry ſhifting *Proteus's*
ſuch *Amphibious Chriſtians*, as can live both in *Land* and *Water*,
Church and *Conventicle*, (and that, more eſpecially, to get *Prey*) will
intirely be defeated of their many baſe Ends ; *Conſcience* ſhall have
its full *Liberty*, but the *State-Libertine* wholly abridg'd from promo-
ting their *Maggotty Commonwealth Innovations* ; or abuſing the *Sacred Robe* of *Magiſtracy*, *for a Cloak* of *Malicioufneſs*, *Avarice*, or
both ; and were this reaſonable diſtinction effectually proſecuted,
and their little factious *Properties* excluded from *voting* the *Sword*
into ſuch unworthy Hands, it muſt fall in courſe to ſome honeſter
Man's Lot, who will be the *Miniſter of God for good*, *and bear it not
in vain*. 'Tis. likewiſe to be hop'd, this may tend by degrees to
the better information of the deluded People, make them reflect
upon the *Inconſiſtency* of their *Principles*, and Unwarrantableneſs of
their *Schiſm*, how naturally they tend to a *licentious Prophanation* of all
things *Sacred* and *Civil*, whilſt Men of *corrupt* Minds can ſo eaſily
proſtitute the moſt *ſolemn Obligations* of *Religion*, and *Conſcience*, to
two ſuch ſervile reſpects as *Intereſt*, and *Humour*. Neither are we
to deſpair, but it may work a *Reformation* in the Perſons themſelves ;
for generally when Men get nothing by acting the *Hypocrite*, they
care no longer to wear the *Vizard*, chuſe rather to appear as they
really are, and fall at laſt to deſire a right Information of Things,
ſince *Error* and *Deceit* has fail'd in thoſe Advantages, which were
formerly the main Support of their *Unrighteous Mammon*. But
whatever the Event be as to them, I am confident you are ſatisfied
no *Government* can be ſafe in ſuch *ſlippery* hands ; for they that can
be *any thing*, will be *every thing*, and are good for *nothing* ; having
betray'd their own *Conſciences*, is it poſſible they ſhould demur ſerving others in the like kind ?

  4*thly*, But to come to that which is moſt conſiderable in this caſe,
indeed the main Support of every *Government* : By this means all
Publick Deliberations, and *Reſolves*, will be carried on in a ſmooth and
even, ſteddy, uniform Courſe, free from *Factious Oppoſitions*, with
the many other by-reſpects of *Intriguing Intereſts* : This, I ſay, in a

great meafure, at leaft, would abate the feveral *Feuds*, ay, and unreafonable *Expences* too, at the *Election of our National Reprefentatives*, and fecure their *Debates*, when *Affembled*, from frequent *Embarafsments*, according to the *French* Term, the *Obftrufkions* and *Delays*, which fuch as cannot obtain their own private, *pettifh Humours*, are prone to interpofe in the moft. weighty *Tranfactions*, tho' never fo prejudicial to the *Common Good*. In like manner all other finifter *Practices*, *Plots*, and *Brangles*, whether in *Towns Corporate*, *City*, or *County*, would be reduc'd to fomething of Temper, *Noife* and *Nonfence* being once excluded, fuch Men in courfe muft come in place, as would fpeak to the purpofe, and act upon a *Principle*. And if any one objects this would be too great an Invafion upon their *Liberties*, I fhall only reply, as at firft, 'tis no more than what their admired Neighbours, the *Hollanders*, did upon their own accord, to prevent the dangerous Confequences of their many *Popular Heats*, and *Tumultuous Affemblies*, when they gave way that all their *Right* thereto fhould be *devolv'd* upon a few fober underftanding Men, who knew better how to act for the *Common Welfare* than themfelves: But whether many, or few (for this propounds only the exclufion of fome, no alteration in the whole *Conftitution*, as well knowing neither *Oligarchy*, nor *Polyarchy* will do with us, however there be zealous Pretenders to both) fo they be all of one Piece, Bufinefs will go on much the fmoother, and be fooner brought to a Conclufion: And therefore give me leave to transferr St. *Paul's* Comparifon, from the *Church* to the *Body Politick*, it being equally dangerous to them both, as in the *Natural*, if the *Head* be a *Monarch*, and the *Feet Commonwealths-men*; the *Eye* of the *Presbyterian*, and the *Ear* of the *Congregational Perfwafion*, with the *Devil* and all of little *Maggotty Sectaries grumbling* in the *Belly*, what care can be taken of the whole? What will become of it in the end? Amongft fundry pretty *Crotchets*, which in the *Low Countries* hang out for *Signs*, there is one at *Harlem*, call'd the *Misforftand*, that is, a *Barrel* of *Beer* between two *Dray-men*, turn'd *Back* to *Back*, and fo pulling two contrary ways; I have known a *Nation* ftanding in this unhappy Pofture for nigh thefe Sixty Years together, with thefe aggravating Circumftances, that as there have been many more than two *Fullers*, fo they pull'd more than Twenty feveral ways, that the poor *Veffel* hath been able to hold out thus long is much; yet that it fhould hold out much longer, will be more to admiration.

5tbly, That the *Monarch*, and *Monarchy*, will be hereby very much fecured, cannot be difputed; for, as we fee, how fatal it is, when a *Prince* differs in his Perfwafion from the *Eftablifh'd Religion*,

fo

fo one of that *Perfwafion* is as little fecure, if his *Miniflers*, with other inferiour *Officers*, and *Dependants*, are of different *Sentiments*, and. *Inclinations*; and that not only as to *Divine*. Matters, but the very *Nature* and *Original* of all *Humane Conftitutions*, and *Civil Societies*; And. whoever wears the *Crown* of *England*, upon any other than the *Old Church* of *England* Principle, will neither find that fit eafie, nor himfelf long fafe; for notwithftanding the many *Proteftations*, and *Acknowledgments*, which either *Flattery*, or *Intereft*, may for fome time, oblige themunto, there is not *One* in *Ten* of the feveral *Factions*, could they have there own Wills, would endure a Monarchy, any more than the *Kingdom* of *Heaven* a *Commonwealth*. That fuch a Book as *Ludlow*'s *Memoirs*, fhould come abroad at this time of day, is fomewhat odd, and argues his *Admirers* Men of no little *Affurance*; yet really however it may prevail upon the infatuated *Sectaries*, the many *Plots* and *Counter-Plots* there difcover'd, their implacable *Enmities* one againft another, perfidious *Hypocrifies*, and clandeftine *Underminings*, with a continued Irrefolution as to any thing of *Accord* and *Settlement*, muft convince every Man of Sence, that (like their *Infernal Abettor*) their fole *Talent* lay in doing *Mifchief*, oppofing, and pulling down; which, having effected, they could no moreagree what fhould fucceed, than the *Mob* of *Capua*, when they had brought things into the fame condition. Read over his whole *Second Volume* with a *ferious* Attention ; and then tell me, whether *Hell* it felf can be reprefented in greater Confufion, than. he doth there the Conduct of *Affairs*, the *Contrafts*, and *Counterminings* of the feveral *Ufurping Powers*, till things being brought to the Extremity of *Diftraction*, with an Expence of *Blood* and *Treafure*, never before paralell'd, they were forc'd, like the *Evil Spirit* in the *Gofpel*, to return from whence they fet out, and ceafe troubling the World, till their former *Freaks*, and its own *Follies* fhould be quite forgot ; yet thefe were our *Commonwealth-Patriots*, the *Keepers* of our *Liberties*, and what not: From whom, and all fuch, *God* keep this poor *Nation* for evermore.

6thly, Were I not fure, you would expect fomething in reference to the *Church* of *England*, I had been wholly filent as to that Point, being of a Perfwafion fomewhat more *fanguin*, than moft of her *Sons*, *Clergy* as well as *Lay*, viz. that what a wife *Obferver* faid of the whole Nation in general, is more applicable here, *None can deftroy her but her felf*. There is, as I hinted juft now, fo ftrick and mutual a dependance between the *Crown* and *Mytre*, that they muft both ftand and fall together : And, give me leave farther to add, we muft never expect a fettled *State*, or continued *Peace*, without keeping them

(22)

them both up, whatever *Diftrufts* fome may lie under, and *Neceffities* others plead; which perhaps themfelves made, to bring in their *New-fangled Devices.* 'Tis true, whenever a *Nation* is fo unhappy as to be divided within it felf, fall into *Parties,* and *Fractions,* upon any account, either *Ecclefiaftical,* or *Civil*; as fome *Church-men* will make themfelves, or be made *Properties* therein, fo the *Church* muft expect to bear her proportion in fuch *Diftractions,* and that to a large degree; yet ftill if the main *Body* keeps fteady to its felf, *walks by the fame Rule, and minds the fame* Thing, fuch a referve of *Mercy* and *Providence* will conftantly attend her, as though *perfecuted,* fhe fhall never be forfaken, caft down, but not deftroy'd; and it very rarely happens fome great *Good* does not come out of that *Evil.* But if fhe forfakes her felf, *folds* her Arms in a carelefs Defpair, or confults her Peace by an *Union* with *Faction* and *Schifm,* and as the Judicious Bifhop *Laney* obferv'd, *pulls down her old Walls,* her *Confeffions of Doctrine,* and *Canons* of *Difcipline* (like the foolifh Trojans) to let in a comprehenfive *Horfe,* full of thofe very Enemies, which have us'd all other means; tho' *God* be prais'd in vain, to effect her ruine; This would be a *Perditio tua ex te,* and as the fame good-Man farther declares, *againft* all the Rules of *Wifdom* and *Government*; by which it was ever thought neceffary, *that the People fhould conform to the Laws of the Church, never that the Church fhould conform to the Humours of the People*; and therefore, as he very well diftinguifhes, to fuch as be content to leave their *Faults* and *Errors* behind them, we ought to fet our *Gates* wide open, and need not pull down our *Walls*; but if they bring their *Errors,* Animofities, and divided Judgments along with them, to admit fuch, only fecures them from Punifhment, but leaves them free to all other *Caufes* of *Diffenfion,* or rather fortifies and animates them to purfue their *Differences with the greater Violence.* God, to be fure, receives none but upon *Repentance* and *Amendment*; and why his *Church* fhould do otherwife, I am yet to learn; if they will not be the fame with us, let them *Herd* by themfelves, and not come among us, their *Room* is better than their *Company:* And therefore I have always fufpected, either want of *Underftanding,* or *Affection,* in thofe Perfons, who trouble their Heads fo much in that *Affair,* without any regard to the *Caution* in the *Gofpel,* as likewife the reafon of the thing, and will be treating with, ay, and courting too, thofe *Wolves,* becaufe they *appear in Sheeps Cloathing*; or can otherwife alledge fome *plaufible Pretences,* which the *Devil* is never without, nor fails of a fupply to fuch as act on his behalf; whereas *Matter of Fact* hath all along fpoke quite the contrary, the continued Experience of nigh an *Hundred Years* moft fadly affur'd us, that they could never

be

Laft Sermon at Court, p. 26.

be oblig'd by any *Kindness*, nor satisfy'd with any *Condescension·*

And, now, Sir, without doubt you must be thoroughly tir'd, and find the Trouble I was *complemented* into, return'd upon your self, receiving a *Volume* instead of a Letter. Yet, be assur'd, 'twas with some difficulty it ended here; for having once set my Thoughts *afloat*, the *Current* ran so strong, I could not *stem* its Force so as to stop at pleasure: And by this you may see confirm'd what I have hitherto entertain'd you withal ; for if a single Person cannot take his *Liberty*, in so little an Affair too, without somewhat of Inconvenience and Trouble, how much worse must it prove in a whole *Body*, a *Community* of *People*, who are so easily hurried on, without knowing what they do, or from whom they act, till all end in *Mischief* and *Confusion* : And therefore give me leave to declare, that the *Restraints* propounded in the *Premises*, whatever satisfaction they may give you, and some few of your *Temper*, will be no ways acceptable to that extravagant *Licentiousness*, both *Corporal*, and *Spiritual*, *Ecclesiastical* and *Civil*, which hath so long had the Ascendant amongst us, and bears too nigh Affinity to that Acknowledgment in *Livy* ; *Nec Morbum ferre possumus, nec Remedium.*

God, in his due time, make us sensible both of the *Folly* and *Danger*, which such Courses tend unto: In the mean while, and ever, continue to defend our *Church* from all her *Enemies, within*, as well as *without* ; the daily Prayer of,

April 6th.
1698.

S I R,

Yours, &c.

——M ——n.

www.ingramcontent.com/pod-product-compliance
Lightning Source LLC
Chambersburg PA
CBHW061240260626
47172CB00003B/947

* 9 7 8 3 3 3 7 3 0 9 1 5 2 *